W9-BRJ-006

HOOEY HIGGINS

and the

Shark

HOOEY · HIGGINS
and the
Shark

HOOEY HIGGINS
and the
Shark

STEVE VOAKE
illustrated by Emma Dodson

CANDLEWICK PRESS

For Jon Voake, with love and thanks
S. V.

For Karim and Farid
E. D.

This is a work of fiction. Names, characters, places, and incidents are either products of the author's imagination or, if real, are used fictitiously.

Text copyright © 2010 by Steve Voake
Illustrations copyright © 2010 by Emma Dodson

All rights reserved. No part of this book may be reproduced, transmitted, or stored in an information retrieval system in any form or by any means, graphic, electronic, or mechanical, including photocopying, taping, and recording, without prior written permission from the publisher.

First U.S. edition 2012

Library of Congress Cataloging-in-Publication Data is available.

Library of Congress Catalog Card Number pending

ISBN 978-0-7636-5782-6

12 13 14 15 16 17 BVG 10 9 8 7 6 5 4 3 2 1

Printed in Berryville, Virginia, U.S.A.

This book was typeset in Stempel Schneidler.
The illustrations were done in ink line and wash.

Candlewick Press
99 Dover Street
Somerville, Massachusetts 02144

visit us at www.candlewick.com

CONTENTS

"Wow!" said Twig. "Would you look at that!"

Hooey stared through the shop window at the gigantic chocolate egg, and his mouth made an **oooh** shape. He felt like an explorer who has spent his whole life searching for the Holy Grail, only to find it in the window of the corner store.

"Twig," he whispered, "that is stupendous."

The doorbell dinged as they entered the shop, and Hooey stopped to gaze at the window display. If anything, the egg looked even more beautiful from this angle. There was a red ribbon around it, tied up in a bow, and without the glass in the way, you could actually smell the chocolate.

"Oh," said Twig, closing his eyes and clasping his hands together, "I think I can hear angels."

"That," said Mr. Danson, pointing to a radio on the counter, "is Classic FM. Helps the customers relax."

He took a couple of Crunchies from the stand and placed them on the counter. "The usual, is it, boys?"

"Thanks, Mr. Danson."

Hooey watched as the shopkeeper arranged the Snickers bars. "That's some egg you've got there."

Mr. Danson stopped moving the sweets around and turned to look at the window display. "Ah, yes, my œuf en chocolat, as the French would say. She's quite something, isn't she? I'm hoping to drum up some more business so I can afford a new shop window."

"Why do you need a new shop window?" asked Twig. "You can see through that one like anything."

"Oh, you can see through it, all right," agreed Mr. Danson. "But what I want is my name etched across the glass, like a true chocolatier."

His eyes glazed over as his fingers moved through the air in front of him.

DEREK DANSON'S DELICIOUS DELICACIES

he said in a hushed voice. "Imagine how that would look."

Imagine, said Twig.

There was silence for a few moments; then Hooey coughed politely. "Um, Mr. Danson, how much would an egg like that cost?" he asked, picking up his Crunchie bar and putting a handful of change on the counter. He thought of the birthday money he still had on his shelf at home. "Would it be more than five pounds?"

Mr. Danson smiled. "I'm afraid so," he said. "Quite a lot more, in fact."

"How much more?" asked Twig.

"About another sixty," said Mr. Danson.

"SIXTY-FIVE POUNDS?" said Twig incredulously. "That's an awful lot of money."

"It's an awful lot of œuf," said Mr. Danson.

* * *

"He's right, you know," said Hooey as they walked along the beach. "It is an awful lot of œuf." The tide was out and he could see the gray April sky reflected in the tide pools. "How long do you think it would last?"

"About a day," said Twig, "and then they'd have to carry me to the ambulance with chocolate poisoning."

Hooey frowned. "Can you get chocolate poisoning?"

"Dunno," said Twig, "but I'm willing to try."

They climbed the steps by the sea wall and made their way through the narrow streets toward home.

"Twig," said Hooey when they reached the end of his road, "I can't stop thinking about that egg."

"Me neither," said Twig.

"How much money have you got?" asked Hooey.

Twig dug deep into his pockets and
pulled out

a half-eaten
chocolate cookie,

a green plastic
grasshopper,

and a few coins.

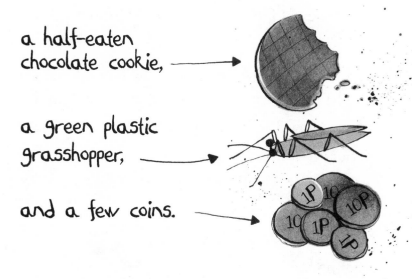

He held out his hand for Hooey to count.

"Thirty-three pence," said Hooey. "Is that it?"

"I've got another ninety-six at home."

"Ninety-six *pence*?" echoed Hooey.

"Don't say it like that. It's very nearly a
pound."

"But we need sixty-five pounds, Twig."

"Well, how much have you got?"

"I've got five pounds left over from my birthday."

"So not really enough, then," said Twig.

"There must be a way of making that kind of money," said Hooey. "We just have to find out what it is."

Twig thought for a moment. "I saw a program about Bill Gates once. He made GAZILLIONS of pounds."

"Not when he was eight years old, Twig."

"Ah, but that's probably just 'cause he never got around to it. Probably had to go shopping with his mum and that."

Hooey
kicked a small stone
and watched it skip along the
pavement. "What's your point, Twig?"

"My point is, we're out of school,
right? We've got loads of time to
make money."

"It can't be that easy, though.
Otherwise everybody'd be doing it."

"That's probably just what Bill
Gates's mum said. And now look
at him. He's probably got whole
rooms full of chocolate. He's
probably sick of it, to be
honest."

9

Hooey imagined the giant egg sitting next to his bed, the smell of chocolate wafting through every room in the house.

"You're right, Twig," he said. "Soon as we think of something, we have to phone each other, OK?"

"OK," said Twig.

Shweet.

Will and Hooey

Grandma
and
Grandpa

Mum
and
Dad

Dingbat

A SHARK IN SHRIMPTON

The Higgins family lived by the sea in a house with one chimney, three floors, and three bedrooms. Mum and Dad slept in one bedroom, Grandma and Grandpa slept across the hallway, and Will and Hooey slept on bunk beds in the attic.

Hooey had actually been christened Thomas Higgins, but everyone called him Hooey because, for the first six months of his life, his brother, Will, kept pointing to his crib and asking, "Who he? Who he?"

After that, the name just kind of stuck.

When Hooey got home, Grandpa was sitting at the kitchen table, reading the newspaper and eating toast and marmalade.

"Want some toast, Hooey?"

"Thanks, Grandpa," said Hooey. Grandpa loved toast, so there was always some around.

As Hooey spread the toast thickly with butter and jam, Dingbat the dog rested his chin on Hooey's leg and looked up with deep longing in his eyes. Hooey guessed Dingbat probably felt the same way about toast as he did about chocolate, so he broke a bit off and fed him under the table.

As Dingbat crunched up the crusts and thumped his tail on the floor, Grandpa peered over the top of his newspaper.

"Hey, Hooey," he said, "listen to this."

"I'm listening," said Hooey. He held out his plate so Dingbat could lick the butter off. "What's going on, Grandpa?"

"It says here that a shark has been seen off the coast of Shrimpton-on-Sea."

"A **SHARK**?" said Hooey, screwing the top back on the jam. "Are you sure?"

Grandpa tapped the newspaper.

"Says it right here in black and white. What d'you think about that, then, eh, Hooey?"

"I think," said Hooey, "that it's a once-in-a-lifetime opportunity."

* * *

After he'd finished his toast, Hooey took
the paper upstairs, where Will was busy
designing something on the back of an old
roll of wallpaper. Will always used wallpaper,
because whenever his designs got too
complicated (and they usually did) he just
unrolled a bit more.

"Hey, Will," said Hooey. "What you
working on?"

"A lion trap," said Will.

"Nice," said Hooey. "What's it for?"

"Catching lions."

"Excellent!"

Hooey looked over Will's shoulder and saw
that he had drawn a picture of a lion. The
lion was cupping one of its ears with a paw
and appeared to be listening to something.
It looked confused, as if it wasn't quite
sure what to do next. Underneath, Will had
underlined the word **LION** to make sure

everyone knew
exactly what they
were dealing
with.

"How's it work,
then?" asked Hooey.

Will unrolled a bit more wallpaper
and Hooey saw that he had drawn a picture
of a truck with the back door open and a
ramp leading up into it. All around it were
speakers of the kind you might see at a
rock concert. Will had drawn lots of wavy
lines to show that there was sound coming
out. In between the lines he had written
DEEP DOG NOISES.

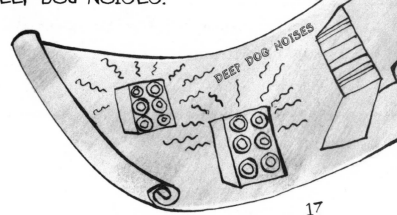

"Now, then," said Will. "Lions are cats, right?"

"Right."

"And cats are frightened of dogs."

"True."

"So all you have to do is record a dog barking, then slow it down."

"Why?"

"So that it makes deep dog noises. Then the lion will think he's being chased by a giant dog and he'll run straight into the trap."

"Will," said Hooey, "you're a genius." He waved the newspaper at him. "Have a break a minute," he said. "Take a look at this."

Will glanced at the paper. "**Vicar Opens Local Flower Show**," he said. "What about it?"

"Not that," said Hooey. "Next to it."

Will looked closer. WHOA!
"A **SHARK**? In Shrimpton?"

"Yup," said Hooey, folding up the newspaper. "You know what that means, don't you?"

"No," said Will. "What?"

"It means we can catch it and collect the reward."

Will stared at the newspaper. "It doesn't say anything about a reward."

"Not yet," said Hooey, "but there's bound to be one. It'll probably be advertised in tomorrow's paper or something."

"Hooey, you can't just go out and catch a shark," said Will, who was two years older than Hooey and knew about these things. "You need to have A Plan."

"A plan!" said Hooey, handing Will a fresh pencil. "Excellent!"

THE WAITING GAME

The next morning, Grandpa was in his bathrobe with a towel draped over one arm when he met Hooey on the landing.

"Are you having a bath, Grandpa?" asked Hooey.

"Well, that was the idea," said Grandpa.

"Can you leave the water in when you've finished?"

"Certainly," replied Grandpa. "Any particular reason?"

"I might want to put a shark in it later," said Hooey.

Grandpa raised an eyebrow. "A shark, eh? That'll be a sight worth seeing."

"I know," agreed Hooey. "We can charge people and everything."

"Well, you've obviously given it some thought," said Grandpa. "I'll go easy on the bubble bath, then, shall I?"

Hooey put his thumbs up. "Thanks Grandpa!"

Twig was very excited when he got the phone call. "A SHARK?" he asked. "Where?"

"In the sea," said Hooey. "Want to help catch it?"

"Course!" said Twig. "Meet you there!"

Although the sun was shining, it was still early, and the beach was empty. Dingbat barked at the waves and ran off to sniff some seaweed.

"Right," said Hooey, snapping the elastic on his red-striped swimming trunks. "Time to put the plan into action."

He held a cricket bat tightly in one hand and gripped a bottle of ketchup in the other.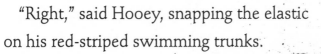

"Are you going to kill it?" asked Twig, holding on to the rope that was tied around Hooey's waist.

"No," said Hooey. "I'm just going to stun it. And when I do, you need to be ready with the net."

Twig frowned. "What net?"

"He means the duvet cover," explained Will, pointing to a bundle of flowery material on the sand.

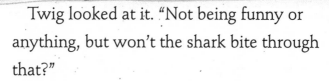

Twig looked at it. "Not being funny or anything, but won't the shark bite through that?"

"Normally, yes," said Will. "But Hooey will have stunned it with the cricket bat, so it won't be able to think straight."

"Right," said Twig. "Gotcha."

Hooey walked toward the waves and felt the rope tighten around his middle. "Not yet, Twig," he called. "Only pull if it looks like I'm drowning."

"How will I know?" asked Twig.

"I'll splash about for a bit and go under," replied Hooey.

Shweet,

said Twig.

Will looked at his watch. "Hooey, it's eight fifty-seven a.m. We need you in the water by nine, remember?"

"OK," said Hooey. He was glad Will was getting involved. Although Will didn't think much of Hooey's ideas, he usually ended up doing the planning.

"OK, everyone," Hooey announced. "I'm going in."

The sea was cold, and as the water came over his trunks, he gave a little squeak.

"Are you OK, Hooey?" called Twig. "Not drowning or anything?"

"No, I'm fine," said Hooey. "Water's a bit chilly, though."

Will scribbled **Bring hot-water bottles** on his wallpaper plan.

"I think I'm deep enough now," called Hooey. "What's next?"

"Hang on," said Will, unrolling the scroll of wallpaper a bit more. "Cricket bat, ketchup, rope . . . Right, here we are." He cupped one hand around his mouth. "OK, HOOEY, TAKE THE TOP OFF THE KETCHUP, AND SHAKE IT AROUND IN CIRCLES."

As Hooey began plopping dollops of ketchup into the sea, Twig said, "Are you sure sharks like ketchup?"

Will nodded. "Everyone likes ketchup."

"My nan doesn't," said Twig.

"Your nan's not a shark," said Will. "Anyway, that's not the point. The point is, when the shark sees the ketchup, it will think **Ooh, blood!** and swim over to have a look. At which point, Hooey will whack it over the head and we can wrap it in the duvet cover. Then we'll take it home, put it in the bath, and charge people fifty pence a look."

"We should charge a pound," said Twig. "It's not every day you get to see a shark in a bath."

"True," said Will. "A pound it is, then."

Twig clasped his hands together and stared out to sea. "Now," he said, nodding wisely, "we play the waiting game."

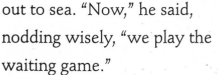

HOOEY'S DISCOVERY

"No sign of him yet," called Hooey. "Shall I put some more ketchup in?"

"Yeah, use the whole thing," said Will. "We've got another bottle at home."

Hooey shook the rest of the ketchup into the water and splashed it around with his hands. Immediately, Twig yanked on the rope and flipped Hooey backward into the sea.

"Twig," spluttered Hooey, "WHAT are you doing?"

"Saving you," said Twig. "You were drowning."

"No, I wasn't," said Hooey, spitting out a mouthful of salty water. "I was mixing up the ketchup."

"Oops," said Twig. "My mistake."

Hooey stood up and scanned the horizon. There was now a family-size serving of ketchup in the sea, and the water around him had turned a reddish pink. He guessed the shark would be along any minute now and secretly hoped it wouldn't bring too many friends.

"Hey!" shouted Twig. "I think I see something!"

Hooey gripped the cricket bat more tightly. "What? What have you seen?"

"I think it's a jellyfish," said Twig.

"A *jellyfish*?" Hooey was worried. They hadn't discussed the possibility of a jellyfish showing up. "Where's the jellyfish?"

"There," said Twig, hopping excitedly from foot to foot. "On your right."

Hooey turned and stared across the water.

"Twig," he said, "it's got MARKET written on it."

"Must be a rare one," said Twig.

"Or a plastic bag," said Hooey.

"Maybe we should just stay quiet for a minute," Will suggested. "If the shark hears us all talking about plastic bags, he might get spooked."

"Or," said Twig, "he might just think we're going about our daily business."

"I doubt it," said Will. "Not with a cricket bat and a bottle of ketchup."

"I really don't think it matters," said Hooey, who was starting to get cold. "Sharks don't understand English."

"The ones who jump through hoops do," said Twig. "I've seen blokes with buckets of fish telling them all kinds of stuff."

"That's dolphins," said Will.

"Same difference," said Twig.

"Except dolphins don't leap out and bite your head off," said Will.

"WHAT?" asked Hooey nervously. "What was that?"

"Relax," said Will. "When was the last time you heard of someone with ketchup and a cricket bat getting their head bitten off by a shark?"

"Umm . . ."

"Exactly. So stop worrying."

Hooey turned back to face the ocean. The water was normally so clear that you could see all the way down to the bottom, but a storm the night before had stirred up the sand. What with that and the blobs of ketchup floating around, it was hard to see anything at all.

As he took a few steps forward, the sand swirled beneath his feet and then, suddenly, something banged against his ankle. "Ow!" he cried, quickly pulling his leg away. "What was that?"

"SHARK!" shouted Twig, and he yanked the rope with both hands.

"Twig, you have *got* to stop doing that!" said Hooey. He took a deep breath and put his head to one side, listening for any underwater swooshing noises that might give the shark's position away.

"Can you see it?" called Twig.

"Not yet," said Hooey.

"Maybe it's swimming upside down so we can't see its fin," Twig suggested.

"Cunning," said Will. "Very cunning."

Hooey waited anxiously for a few moments.

"Maybe it wasn't a shark," he said, peering into the water.

"What?" exclaimed Twig unhappily. "Not even a small one?"

"Don't think so," said Hooey. He stuck his leg out and waved it about a bit in case the shark needed some encouragement. Then he turned and shook his head. "No, there's nothing there. Ooh, hang on a minute."

Hooey's foot had struck something hard, but it didn't feel snappy or bitey enough to be shark's teeth. "Hold on," he said. "I'm going to investigate."

Holding his breath, he flipped forward and swam down to the bottom.

The salt stung his eyes, but he could just make out a **HUGE** spiky object, shaped like a giant chestnut, lying on the bottom. "Hey, everyone!" he shouted as he splashed back up to the surface. "I think I've just found the world's biggest sea urchin!"

URCHIN ENTERPRISES

"I can only find one snorkel," said Twig,
rummaging around in the back of his garage.
"Ooh, wait. And a pair of flippers."
He stood up, flapped them together, and
made a barking noise like a seal.

Dingbat ran around in circles, excitedly
barking back, before finding some old boots in
the corner that needed sniffing.

"No more masks, then?" asked Hooey, who
was holding the only one they had found.

"'Fraid not," said Twig, scrabbling through
another drawer, "although I can set you up
with some nice gardening gloves in green."

"No, thanks," said Hooey.

"Hang on," said Will, holding up an old plastic fish tank. "How about this? It could be like one of those viewing windows." He stuck his head in and peered through. "See? People could look at the sea urchin without having to swim down."

"Brilliant," said Hooey. "And I got a badge-making kit for my birthday. We could sell badges that say:

"Good thinking," said Will. "What we need now is some Careful Planning."

"Careful planning!" said Hooey. "Excellent!"

*   *   *

Back at Hooey and Will's house, Twig helped Grandpa make extra toast while Hooey and Will set up the badge-making kit on the kitchen table. Dingbat plodded happily up and down, gobbling up any crumbs that fell on the floor.

"Hello, my boys," said Grandma as she wandered through in search of her knitting. "Is someone making toast?"

"I am," said Twig. "Want a slice?"

"Better make it two," said Grandma. "I'm playing *World of Warcraft* with Mrs. Jenkins this afternoon. She keeps getting us lost in the dungeon, so I need to keep my strength up."

"Don't overdo it, Iris," said Grandpa, patting her arm. "You know how those trolls upset you."

39

Hooey sat next to Will and saw that he'd drawn a big green ball with spikes coming out of it. At the bottom of the paper there were lots of cartoon people with their hands in the air and their mouths forming big Os of amazement. Along the top, in bright red letters, were the words:

COME AND SEE
THE WORLD'S BIGGESTEST
SEA URCHIN
£1 A LOOK

Urchin Enterprises

"**Wow!**" said Twig excitedly. "I am *definitely* paying to see that."

"You don't have to, Twig," said Hooey. "Staff members get in free."

Twig was so overcome that he had to put down the butter knife and lean on the kitchen counter. "You won't regret this," he said.

"Do you want to come, Grandpa?" asked Hooey.

"I'd love to," said Grandpa, "but it would have to be this afternoon. I promised Alfie Rossiter I'd help him plant his potatoes."

"No problem," said Hooey. "Tell Alfie we'll throw in a free badge if he wants to come too."

"Stop giving stuff away, Hooey. You'll eat into our profits," said Will, reaching for the green felt pen.

"Sorry," said Hooey. He waited until Will looked back at his drawing, then quietly held up a badge, pointed to it, and nodded at Grandpa. Grandpa smiled and put his thumb up. As Will glanced up from his drawing, Hooey dropped the badge and smiled sweetly.

"What?" asked Will.

"Nothing," said Hooey.

When Grandpa had gone to the community garden and Grandma and Mrs. Jenkins were busy blasting each other on the computer, Will said, "I think there's one more thing we need to make sure we get enough customers."

"What's that?" asked Hooey.

"A sandwich board."

"I expect people will bring their own," said Twig.

"No," said Will patiently. "Not sandwiches. A sandwich *board*. It's what people use to advertise things. You get two big pieces of cardboard and you write down whatever it is you're advertising. Then you stick one on either side of you and walk up and down for a while. What d'you think, Twig? You up for it?"

"Hmm, I dunno," said Twig. "I won't look stupid or anything, will I?"

"No way!" said Will. "All the marketing executives do it." He winked at Hooey and then unrolled his wallpaper to show him a detailed drawing he had done. Hooey bit his lip and concentrated hard on not laughing.

"Twig," he said at last. "I think you're about to make a lot of people very happy."

TWIG'S NEW OUTFIT

"This had better be worth it," said Twig, "because I feel like a right donut."

"You look brilliant," said Hooey as Dingbat pressed his nose against the window of **BOB BABBINGTON'S BOUNTIFUL BAKERY.** "And anyway, you're supposed to draw attention to yourself. That's the whole point."

Twig stood in the middle of Main Street wearing two large pieces of cardboard that had been strapped to him with several lengths of white underwear elastic, borrowed from Grandma's sewing chest. This had the effect of making the cardboard bounce up and down as he walked, as if the whole thing was on springs.

The sign on
his front said:

And the sign
on his back said:

"It's not the sign so much," said Twig, pausing to look at his reflection in the window. "It's all this other stuff."

Hooey had to admit that Twig had a point. Although the drinking straws taped to his head looked very effective, the felt pen used to color his face had turned a sort of luminous green, giving him the appearance of some weird garden vegetable.

But at least it made people stop and stare.

Quite a lot of them were doing it now, in fact.

"**Uh-oh**," said Twig suddenly. "Look out. It's Big Bazzer."

Walking toward them was a large, scowling boy, his fists half-clenched as if they were squeezing a couple of invisible bananas. His hair was shaved at the sides and what was left had been dyed yellow-blond, so it looked as if a small field of stubble was sprouting from the top of his head. He had the word BAZ written across his knuckles in blue ink, which Twig said was a reminder for when Miss Troutson took attendance.

"Don't worry," said Hooey. "As long as you don't call him Basbo, you'll be fine."

"I won't," said Twig. "He's been after me for ages."

"Why?" asked Will.

"Because of the poster competition—the antibullying one." Twig stared nervously at the approaching Bazzer. "Don't you remember? His slogan was

BEAT THE BULLIES—POUND 'EM INTO THE GROUND

and when he showed it in assembly, I burst out laughing. Then my poster went and won."

"What did yours say?"

"Don't Be Unfair—Just Care and Share."

"No wonder he wants to kill you," said Hooey.

Twig flattened himself against the wall in an effort not to be seen, but the fact that he was painted bright green, wearing a sandwich board, and had bendy straws sticking out of his head made it rather difficult.

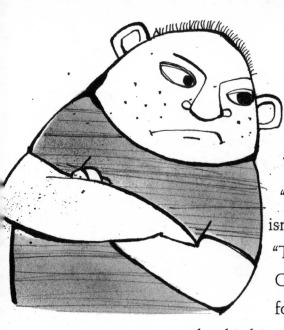

"Well look who it isn't," said Bazzer. "The Laughing Care Bear." He folded his arms so that his biceps bulged out of his T-shirt. "Not laughing now, is we?"

"I wasn't laughing in the first place," said Twig. "I had a fly up my nose."

"Probably just trying to blow it out," said Hooey, screwing up his nose to demonstrate. "Fnuuuhh! Like that."

"Do you fink I'm a total idiot?" said Bazzer, taking a step closer to Twig. "You're not talking your way out of this one. I'm gonna wazz you up and fwap you in the bongers. And you know why, Twiglet?"

Twig looked around as if expecting to see the answer taped to a passerby. "Umm . . . because you like fwapping stuff?"

"No." Bazzer squeezed his knuckles until they cracked. "Because you made me look like a complete grimble, that's why."

"No, I didn't," said Twig suddenly. "You did that all by yourself . . .

BASBO.

There was a moment's silence.

Twig gulped loudly.

Then, as Bazzer raised his fist,
Dingbat shot out of **BOB BABBINGTON'S BOUNTIFUL BAKERY** with
a sausage roll in
his mouth
and ran after Twig, who
was already squealing
down the road with the
sandwich board bouncing
up and down as he
went.

"Oi!"

yelled Bazzer. "Come
back, y'little frambit!"
Twig took a sudden left
into Marks & Spencer,
followed closely by an
angry Bazzer.

Dingbat was so excited that he flew in after them, got tangled up with the security guard, and flipped him back into a rack of pink nighties.

The guard was still flailing around when Hooey and Will came crashing through the doors.

"HEY!" he shouted. "NO DOGS ALLOWED!"

Will went left and Hooey and Dingbat kept on running, skidding across the floor toward the bathrobes, where Twig was trying to hide behind a mannequin.

"Twig," hissed Hooey, pointing at the boards sticking out on either side of him. "He's going to see you!"

Twig looked around frantically for a few moments, then seemed to relax. "Don't worry," he said. "I think we lost him."

At which point, Bazzer
appeared from behind the
pillar.

Twig screamed, jumped
up, and ran smack-bang into a
mirror. He groaned, clutched
his sandwich board, and
wobbled off toward the
underwear section.

"This wasn't in The Plan,"
said Will, popping his head
through a rack of easy-care dresses.

"This was never in The Plan."

"Hang on," said Hooey. "He's
getting away."

Twig was now sprinting
through the underwear section,
his knees bumping frantically
against the sandwich board as
he headed for the doors.

"Go for it, Twiggy-boy," shouted Will, clapping his hands. "You can do it!"

He might have, too, if it hadn't been for the shop assistant who chose that moment to walk across the aisle carrying a huge armful of underwear. As Twig tried to slow down, his legs seemed to go in several directions at once, and, just for a second, he appeared to be dancing magically above the ground. Then he tripped over his own feet, hit the shop assistant with a loud **ooooffff,** and they both tumbled to the floor in a flurry of bras and underwear.

As people put down their baskets to look, Hooey turned to see Bazzer steaming at full pelt down the aisle, his face bright red with fury.

The sight of all these unusual and interesting things was too much for Dingbat. Deciding they needed immediate investigation, he took off across the floor like a furry bullet, unaware that Hooey still had hold of his leash. As he reached the end of it, the leash twanged like a piece of cheese wire.

YELP!

Dingbat gave a strangled yelp, and Bazzer tripped over the leash with such force that, even as he flew horizontally

through the air, Hooey could tell he wouldn't
be landing before reaching the food
department. Hooey just had time to read
the words THESE ARE NOT JUST
TRIFLES; THESE ARE M&S TRIFLES
before Bazzer cracked his head on
the sign, bounced off the refrigerated display
case, and plunged headfirst into the desserts,
sending whipped cream exploding into the
faces of Saturday shoppers.

Twig began running back up the aisle toward the doors, bras dangling from his ears and a pair of frilly white underwear on his head.

"I don't know about you, Joan," said Mrs. Woodchuck as Twig shot past her, "but I can't keep up with what the young'uns are wearing these days."

"Well, I think it suits him," said Joan.

"RUN!" shouted Twig as Dingbat skidded after him. "Run for your lives!"

Hooey just caught sight of the security guard hauling Bazzer out of the trifles before Will grabbed his arm, and then they were both running after Twig, past the tights and the hats and the three-for-two offers and all the way out of the door to safety.

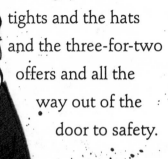

61

SEARCHIN'
FOR THE URCHIN

"**THAT'S IT,**" wheezed Twig, pulling the frilly underpants off his head and throwing them into the sea. "I'm finished."

He shook his head and watched them sink beneath the waves. "I've been traumatized in the underwear department of Marks and Spencer."

"You'll get over it," said Hooey. "Anyway, you definitely got yourself noticed. It's good for business. Maybe you should go and walk around a bit."

"Maybe *you* should go and walk around a bit," said Twig, pulling broken straws from his forehead.

"Hang on," said Will. "I think we might have our first customer."

They all turned to watch Samantha Curbitt walking across the sand toward them. She was blowing a big pink bubble and playing keepie-uppie with a soccer ball.

"Oh, no!" said Twig in a low, panicky whisper. "What am I going to do now?"

Will frowned. "What d'you mean, what are you going to do?"

"It's *Samantha Curbitt*," Twig hissed. "And I'm dressed as a sea urchin!"

"So?"

Twig blushed.

"Oh, I get it." Hooey grinned. "Twig loves Samantha."

"No, I don't," said Twig indignantly. "I do *not*."

"He does," said Hooey.

Samantha popped her bubble gum, trapped the ball under her foot, and smiled. "Nice outfit," she said. "My mum's got that bra. Doesn't usually wear it on her head though."

Hooey tried not to snigger. "Tell her about our plan, Twig."

"Er," said Twig, blushing deeply beneath the green felt pen. "Well, I errr, ummmm . . ."

"What Twig is *trying* to say," said Hooey, "is that we've found a giant sea urchin."

"Really?" asked Samantha. "Can I see it?"

"Sure," said Hooey. "You'll have to pay, though."

"How much?"

Twig twizzled around and pointed to the price on his sandwich board.

"A pound?" said Samantha. "That's a lot of money."

"Not when you consider the cost of the equipment," said Hooey.

Samantha narrowed her eyes. "What equipment?"

Hooey held up the fish tank and rapped it with his knuckles.

"See? State-of-the-art underwater viewing station."

"Plus," said Will, "you get a free badge."

"Let's have a look," said Samantha.

Will rummaged around in the bag and handed her a badge.

Twig smiled shyly. "It says, '**I have seen the Sea Urchin of Shrimpton-on-Sea**.'"

"Yes, thank you, Twig," replied Samantha icily. "I *can* read. Tell you what," she said, tapping the badge against her front teeth, "I'll give you fifty."

"**FIFTY POUNDS!**" exclaimed Twig, dancing around so that the sandwich board bumped against his knees. "That means we're almost there!"

"Fifty *pence*." Samantha corrected him. "And that's my final offer."

"Oh," said Twig.

"Done," said Hooey. He turned to Will.

"William, if you would like to help the lady into her wave-proof apparatus, I shall go prepare the viewing window."

"Viewing window?" said Samantha. "Wave-proof apparatus?"

"Fish tank and wellie boots," said Will.

Twig grinned and held up a pair of mud-spattered wellies. "Shall I help you into them?"

"Save it, NUMPTY," snapped Samantha, taking her shoes and socks off and rolling up her jeans. "I'm going in like this."

"Hey!" protested Will as she skipped over the waves. "You haven't paid yet!"

Samantha waded through the waves until she was standing next to Hooey with water up to her chest.

"You've got to admit it," said Twig admiringly. "That girl has plenty of spirit."

"Let's hope she's got plenty of money, too," said Will.

In the water, Hooey was looking at the waves lapping beneath Samantha's chin.

"Not bothering with the safety gear, then?
Can't say I blame you. I think we need taller
wellies."

He pushed the fish tank into the water and
peered through. The tide was coming in, and
the sea urchin was quite a long way out, but
he could still see it, lurking on the bottom in a
giant-sea-urchiny sort of way. "Look," he said,
passing the fish tank over to Samantha. "See?"

"Where?"

"Up in the sky," said Hooey. "Where d'you
think?"

Samantha gripped the sides of the fish tank and put her head in.

"I can't see a thing," said Samantha. Her voice sounded echoey, as if her head was stuck down a toilet.

"Over to your left," said Hooey.

"Oh, yeah," said Samantha. "Now I see it."

"So, what d'you think?" asked Hooey as

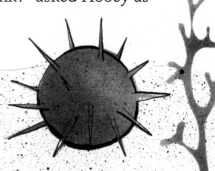

Samantha removed her head from the fish tank. "Bit of a WHOPPER, eh?"

"Well it's *quite* big," said Samantha, "but I wouldn't call it *giant*."

Hooey stuck his head back into the tank. "The water's a bit cloudy," he said. "Maybe we should wait until it clears."

"*You* can wait until it clears. I'm going in. I'm freezing."

"Wait," called Hooey. "Come back!" But Samantha was already wading out of the water and heading up the beach.

"Hi, Samantha," said Twig, back on shore. He held out her shoes with a big, beaming smile. "I shook the sand out for you." Then he turned to Will and whispered, "*No one likes sand in their shoes.*"

"Give me those," said Samantha, snatching them back.

"I trust you enjoyed your sea-urchin experience, Samantha," said Will, holding out his hand. "That'll be fifty pence, please."

"Fifty pence? For WHAT?"

"For the, um, for the sea-urchin experience."

"You expect me to pay fifty pence for standing up to my neck in freezing-cold water and looking through a plastic fish tank at a gray blob half a mile away?"

"Well, if you want to put it that way," said Will, "then, yes."

"DREAM ON," said Samantha, and she stomped off up the beach.

"Hey!" called Twig. "Don't forget your soccer ball!" He ran across the sand and booted the ball as hard as he could.

It spun off the side of his foot, curved up into the air, and landed with a splash in the water. As they watched, the wind carried it over the tops of the waves and out into the gray sea beyond.

"Uh-oh," said Twig. "Don't think that one's coming back."

"Neither's Samantha," said Will.

"What's going on?" asked Hooey, splashing onto the sand.

"Samantha wouldn't cough up," said Will. "Some people just don't know a star attraction when they see one."

"She *is* a star attraction," said Twig dreamily. "Anyway, looks like we've got more customers."

Hooey and Will turned to see two old men walking toward them across the sand.

"It's Grandpa!" exclaimed Hooey. "And he's brought Alfie Rossiter with him!"

"Hello, lads," said Grandpa. "We've only done about half the spuds. But when I told Alfie about your sea urchin, he couldn't wait to come and see it, could you, Alfie?"

Alfie leaned on his walking stick and grinned. "I can see me taters any day of the week," he said. "But we don't get too many giant sea urchins up at the garden."

"I'm afraid there's only one pair of wellies," said Hooey. "And they're not much good once the water's up to your neck."

"We didn't really think that part through," whispered Twig.

Alfie turned to look at Twig's green face and frowned. "Who's he?"

"That's Twig," Hooey explained. "He's pretending to be a sea urchin. For publicity purposes."

"Ah, well," said Alfie. "That's all right, then."

"It's **NOT** all right!" said Will bitterly.
"I should have seen the problem with the
wellies right from the start. I should have
Planned Ahead!"

"It's lucky *we* did, then," said Grandpa.

"What d'you mean?" asked Will.

"This," said Grandpa.

And before they knew it, Grandpa and Alfie
Rossiter had unhitched their suspenders and
dropped their trousers to reveal two pairs of
baggy red, white, and blue
swimming trunks.

"Snap!" said Grandpa. "Britannia rules the waves."

"I bought twenty of them at a fantastic discount at the souvenir shop in town," said Alfie. "Always knew they'd come in handy one day."

"Now, that's what I call Planning!" said Will. As he unrolled his wallpaper plan and wrote **Bring extra swimming trunks,** Grandpa handed him a five-pound note.

"There you go, Will," he said. "Don't forget to save us some chocolate from that egg."

"I won't!" said Will. "Thanks, Grandpa!"

"Come on, then, Alfie," said Grandpa as they waded into the sea after Hooey. "Let's go searchin' for the urchin."

"It's over here somewhere," said Hooey, peering into the fish tank. "Ah, yes, behold the Giant Sea Urchin!"

He passed the tank to Grandpa, who wiped water from his eyes and bent over it.

"Well, Hooey, old boy," he said after a while. "There's definitely *something* down there, but to be honest my eyesight's not what it used to be. I should've brought me specs."

"Oh, give it here," said Alfie, who'd been doing a little dance to keep warm. "Let's have a look."

He gazed into the tank. "Ah, yes. Got it," he said. "Wait a minute, if I can just . . . that's it . . . I can . . . Oh, blimey. Is that . . . ?"

Hooey frowned and looked at Grandpa.

Grandpa looked at Alfie. "What is it, Alfie?" he asked. "What's the matter?"

"We have to get out of the water," said
Alfie. "We have to get out of the water

BOOM BANG-A-BANG

"So," said Mum as they all sat down for dinner, "has everyone had an interesting day?"

"Not bad," said Hooey. "We tried to catch a shark, actually."

"A shark?" said Dad. "That does sound interesting. Any luck?"

"Not much," said Hooey, "but we did find a giant sea urchin."

"Really?" asked Mum.

"Well, yes and no," said Will. "*Yes* because we thought it was one, and *no* because it wasn't."

"What was it, then?"

Hooey looked at Grandpa. "D'you want to tell them, Grandpa?"

Grandpa coughed and looked at his dinner.

"Dad?" said Mum.

"Well," said Grandpa, "it wasn't so much a giant sea urchin as a Second World War mine. Still is, as a matter of fact."

Mum's mouth fell open and she dropped the spoon into the roasted potatoes. "A Second World War mine? But isn't that dangerous?"

"You could say that," said Grandpa, "seeing as how it's packed full of high explosives."

"It was dead exciting, though," said Hooey, warming to the subject. "We thought Alfie had seen a great white shark, so everyone pegged it up the beach to get the cricket bat. But then Alfie told us it was a mine, and we all piled down to the police station. They said that some army divers are going to blow it up tonight. Can we go watch, Mum? Can we, Mum, please?"

"Absolutely not," said Mum, making her No-Way-Don't-Even-Think-About-It face.

"Oh, *puh-leeeease*," said Hooey and Will together.

"I'm sure it'll be OK, love," said Dad, pointing at the crowds of people walking past the window. "After all, it looks as though the whole village is going down to watch."

* * *

There was a carnival atmosphere down on
the seafront. Mrs. Jenkins was dressed as a
Royal Navy commander and staring out to sea
through a rusty old telescope, Alfie Rossiter
was waving his Union Jack shorts over his
head shouting "God save the Queen!" and
Grandma was pushing around a trolley
loaded with tea and currant buns.

The police had cordoned off the beach, and an army Land Rover was driving up and down on the sand, making sure that no one got too close.

"How cool is this?" said Twig.

"We should be charging people," said Will. "We could have made a fortune."

"I just hope that shark's not around," said Hooey. "If he is, he's in for a bit of a shock."

"Crackety-boom!" said Twig. "Biggest flying fish in history."

"TWO MINUTES TO GO," said a policeman with a clipboard and a megaphone. "EVERYONE STAND WELL BACK."

Everyone moved a bit closer. Dingbat stuck his nose through the railings and Hooey, Will, and Twig climbed onto the first rung to get a better look.

"How long now?" asked Hooey.

Will looked at his watch. "About twenty seconds."

"Ooh," said Twig. "How long now?"

Will raised his eyebrows. "About nineteen."

"The suspense is killing me," said Twig.

"Ten seconds," said Will. "Let's count!"

"TEN," said Hooey, Will, and Twig.

"NINE," went the rest of the crowd.

"EIGHT . . . SEVEN . . .
SIX . . . FIVE . . .
FOUR . . . THREE . . .
TWO . . . ONE. . . ."

Everyone held their breath, and for a
moment there was silence.

Then a loud thump shook the ground.
It was followed by a low, rumbling boom,
and suddenly the surface of the sea erupted
into a white pillar of water, which shot up
into the sky, growing higher and higher as
the sea foamed and boiled beneath it.

went the crowd.

said Twig.

"What's that up there?" asked Hooey.

Everyone looked up. There, high in the sky, was a tiny black dot.

"It's the shark!" said Twig excitedly. "It's the **SHARK**!"

"It can't be," said Hooey. "It's not even shark-shaped."

"Well, it was a big explosion," said Twig. "The shark could be all sorts of shapes by now."

"Look!" said Will as the object began falling toward the village. "It's coming in to land!"

"Come on!" said Hooey, jumping down from the railings. "Let's go and see!"

As they ran up the street, there was a loud crash and the sound of breaking glass.

"What was *that*?" asked Twig.

"It came from over there!" cried Hooey.

They flew around the corner, skidded to a halt, and stared at Mr. Danson's shop. The window had been smashed to pieces, and the sidewalk was covered with bits of broken glass.

"Oh, no," said Hooey. "Look!"

Beyond the space where the shop window used to be was a space where the chocolate egg used to be.

And in the space where the chocolate egg used to be, there was Samantha Curbitt's exploded soccer ball.

THE FABULOUS
FISH FLINGERS

"You mustn't blame yourself, Twig," said Hooey as the bell dinged and they walked into the shop.

"No," said Will. "We can do that for you."

"D'you think Mr. Danson is going to be cross?" asked Twig nervously.

"Let's put it this way," said Will. "If he comes out holding a big mallet, it won't be because he's going camping."

"Uh-oh," said Hooey. "Here he comes."

"Bonsoir, boys," said Mr. Danson, emerging from the back room. "Did you hear that smashing noise? It sounded really close."

"I think it *was* really close," said Hooey. They all winced as Mr. Danson turned to look at his smashed-up window display. The egg had been knocked backward and was in hundreds of pieces on the floor.

"My shop window!" he gasped. "My beautiful œuf en chocolat!"

"Sorry, Mr. Danson," said Twig. "I think it was partly my f—"

But Mr. Danson wasn't listening. "My shop window!" he said again. Then he began to smile. "My shop window . . ."

"Mr. Danson," said Hooey, "are you all right?"

"Won't be a sec," said Mr. Danson. Then he disappeared off into the back room.

"Must have been the shock," said Will.

"Shock window," said Twig.

Hooey went over and picked up a piece of the broken egg. "Look," he said, "the chocolate's still OK. Maybe we could help Mr. Danson by picking it up for him."

"Good idea," said Will. He went behind the counter and returned with three plastic bags.

By the time Mr. Danson came back, they had collected a whole bag each.

"There you go, Mr. Danson," said Hooey. "Three bags of quality chocolate."

"We could stick them back together if you like," offered Twig. "I've got some tape at home."

"That's very kind of you," said Mr. Danson, "but there's really no need." Seeing the boys' puzzled expressions, he added, "I've just been on the phone to my insurance company. They've told me I can have the money for a brand-new shop window."

"So you're not cross, then?" asked Twig.

"Cross? Why would I be cross? Now I can show that Bountiful Bob what style really is. I can have the best shop window in the whole of Shrimpton!"

"But what about the egg?" asked Hooey. "It's all smashed to pieces."

Mr. Danson smiled. "They're going to pay for that, too. And you know what that means, don't you, boys?" He nodded at the bags on the counter.

Twig frowned. "You're going to buy some new bags?"

"No," said Mr Danson, smiling so broadly his teeth gleamed. "It means I need to find a good home for all this chocolat."

"I wonder how much chocolate you have to eat before you explode," said Hooey, watching Dingbat chase some seagulls up the beach.

"I don't know," said Twig, stuffing another handful into his mouth,

"but it might come in handy next time I see Basbo. Self-defense and all that."

"Don't worry," said Will. "His mum's grounded him. Something to do with causing criminal damage in Marks and Spencer."

Hooey grinned. "That'll teach him to mess with us."

"To be honest, I don't even care if he kills me now," said Twig. "Just seeing him facedown in custard means I can die a happy man."

"Hey, look," said Will, pointing down to the water's edge. "There's Samantha."

"Oh, yay!" said Twig enthusiastically. "I can go give her the ball back."

"Are you sure that's a good idea?" asked Hooey, looking at what was left of the ball. "It's a bit . . . deflated."

"Nah, it's fine," said Twig. "Just needs a bit of air in it, that's all."

As they watched him scamper down the beach, Hooey asked, "What are those silver things on the sand?"

"Fish," said Will. "The explosion must have blown them out of the water."

"Look," said Hooey. "Samantha's picking one up."

"Uh-oh," said Will. "That doesn't look good."

As they watched, Twig held the deflated ball out to Samantha. Samantha snatched it with her left hand and threw it down onto the sand. Then, with her right hand, she swung the fish around in a wide arc until it struck Twig with a loud **thwaack** on the side of his face.

"Oooooh!" cried Hooey and Will as Twig's feet lifted off the ground and he flopped sideways into the water.

"He was right about one thing," said Will as Samantha dusted her hands together and walked off up the beach. "That girl *has* got plenty of spirit."

They ran down to the water's edge, where Twig was busy tipping seawater out of his shoes. When he saw them, he looked up and smiled.

"I think she likes me," he said.

It wasn't until the sun had turned red and started to sink into the sea that Hooey thought of the Fabulous Fish-Flinging Game.

"All you have to do," he explained, "is grab a fish by its tail and fling it out to sea."

"Sounds good to me," said Will, picking up a fish. "Any special rules?"

"Only one," said Hooey. "Whoever flings their fish the farthest is the Fish-Flinging Champion."

"Shweet," said Twig. "I call first."

"Hang on," said Will. "We should all go at the same time. That way we can see which fish goes the farthest."

"Oh, yeah," said Twig, picking up a large mackerel. "Ready?"

"After three," said Hooey.

"One . . . two . . . THREE!"

At the same moment, they all threw
their fish high into the air, watching them
glitter in the fading sunlight. But as the first
one fell, the sea suddenly seemed to break
open, and a huge pair of jaws rose above the
surface. As the three boys watched in
amazement, the jaws opened wide,
swallowed the fish whole, and
quickly snapped shut again. Then,
with a huge splash, they disappeared
beneath the waves.

"Did you see that?"
squeaked Twig. "It was
the shark! The shark came
and ate our fish!"

For several seconds they all stood open-mouthed, staring at the patch of water where the shark had been only moments before.

"Right," said Hooey at last. "We're going to need a rope, some ketchup, and a cricket bat. Will, are you in?"

"Oh, I'm in," said Will. "I am *definitely* in."

"Let's go!" said Hooey.

"Shweet," said Twig.

They ran across the sand and up the steps, the sound of their laughter fading into the narrow streets until at last the beach was silent once more. All that could be heard was the gentle splash of something big, blue, and shark-shaped swimming out toward the open sea. . . .

. . . with what looked like a pair of frilly white underpants hooked onto the end of its tail.